CH00840203

A DORLING KINDERSLEY BOOK

For Thomas - AG
To Ryan - NM

First published in Great Britain in 1997 by Dorling Kindersley Limited,
9 Henrietta Street, London WC2E 8PS

Reprinted 1999

Visit us on the World Wide Web at
http://www.dk.com

Text copyright © 1997 Alan Garner
Illustrations copyright © 1997 Norman Messenger

A CIP catalogue record for this book is available from the British Library.

ISBN 0-7513-7037-1

Colour reproduction by Dot Gradations
Printed and bound by Tien Wah Press, Singapore

The Little Red Hen

Told by Alan Garner

Illustrated by Norman Messenger

DK

DORLING KINDERSLEY

London • New York • Moscow • Stuttgart

ONCE UPON A TIME

and a good time it was,
a cat, a rat, and a little
red hen lived together
in a house.

The cat had a basket,

the rat had a hole,

and the little red
hen had a strong
wooden perch.

One fine morning
the little red hen said,
"Who'll get up and
light the fire?"

"Not I," said the cat.

"Not I,"  said the rat.

"I'll do it myself," said the little red hen.

So she got up and lit the fire.

Then she said,
"Who'll get up and
make the breakfast?"

"Not I," said the cat.

"Not I,"  said the rat.

"I'll do it myself," said the little
red hen. So she made the breakfast.

Then she said,
"Who'll get up and
eat the breakfast?"

"I will!" said the cat.

"I will!"  said the rat.

"I'll do it myself!"

said the little red hen.

And she ate up the breakfast.

What should she see then coming down the road but a big brown fox carrying a wide white sack.

"Here's a big brown fox," said the little red hen, "with a wide white sack."

And the cat
jumped into its basket,

and the rat ran
into its hole,

so the little red hen
flew up to her strong
wooden perch.

In came the big
brown fox.

"Good day to you,
little red hen," he said.
  "Waltz you down and
        scratch my back."

"Very well," said the
little red hen.

And she waltzed down to scratch, but he caught hold of her, put her in his wide white sack, and away with him.

Now it was a hot day,
and soon he got tired.

So he lay down
under the shadow of
a rock and went
to sleep.

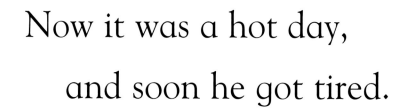

And the little red hen took her scissors
and a needle and thread from under
her wing, and she cut a hole in the
wide white sack,
and out she
got, and . . .

... put a great green stone in her place, and

sewed up the hole,
and away with her.

After a bit, the big brown
fox woke up and put
his wide white sack
on his back and
started off again.

"Much good that rest
has done me!" said he.
"Why, she feels heavier
now than before!"

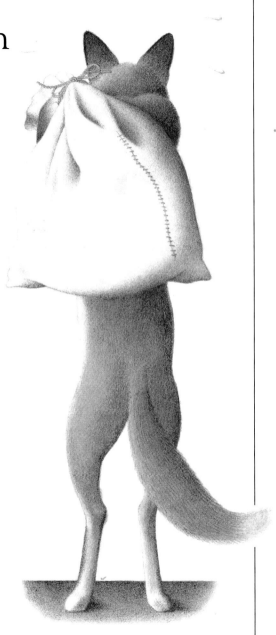

No matter, the big brown fox got home at last, and he told his old grey mother, "Just you get ready the family glass pot, Ma, for I've the little red hen here in the wide white sack."

So the big brown fox's old grey mother got out the family glass pot, filled it with water, and put it on the fire to cook the little red hen.

Now the family glass pot was so fat
that it filled the fireplace right up, and
the big brown fox had to go out and

climb on the roof and tip the wide
white sack down the dim dark chimney.

And so he did.

And the great green stone fell out of the wide white sack down the dim dark chimney and knocked the family glass pot into smithereens and

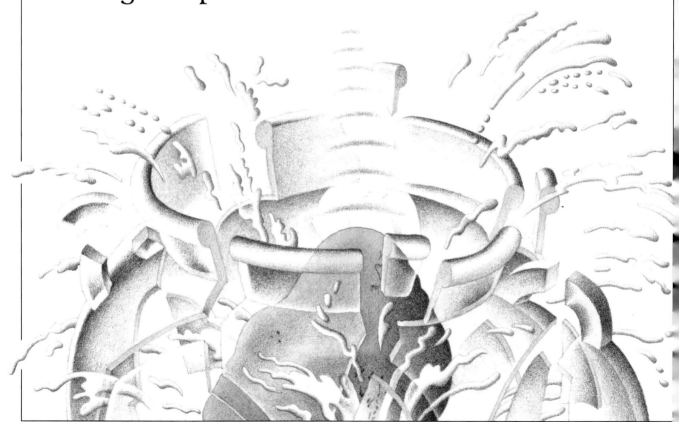

scalded the old grey
mother. She took off
her wooden shoe and
knocked her big brown son off

the roof with it.

"And," said the little red hen to the cat and the rat, "that's that."